DRACULA'S
DEATH

DRACULA'S DEATH

Illustrated by **JÓZSEF SVÁB**
Translated by **LÁSZLÓ TAMÁSFI**

THE DEVIL FLEW AWAY
THE HISTORY OF DRACULA'S DEATH

Written by **LÁSZLÓ TAMÁSFI**
Edited by **ERIKA ROMERO**

Layout editor: Jana Horváth

ISBN 9781736386613
Library of Congress Control Number: 2020925548

Strangers From Nowhere Publishing
www.strangersfromnowhere.com

ABOUT THE BOOK

The original *Dracula's Death* was a slim, pocket-sized Hungarian book published in 1924. It was a "fantastical film-novel" — today we would call it a novelization— based on a silent film released just the year prior.

The movie, also titled *Dracula's Death*, was not an adaptation of Bram Stoker's novel, but an original story written and directed by Károly Lajthay. While it featured the famous vampire, its lead character was Mary, a poor seamstress, who encountered Dracula during her stay at a mental asylum. Austrian actor Paul Askonas played the title role, and wore special effects makeup to transform into a devil-like figure. Mary was played by Hungarian actress Margit Lux. The film was completed in 1921, and premiered two years later, on April 28, 1923 in Budapest.

Unfortunately — just as is the case with a staggering 75% of movies made before 1929— there are no surviving copies of it. All that's left are a handful of photographs, newspaper articles, and this prose adaptation.

Here, we present an English translation of the full Hungarian text, in the hopes that today's audiences will enjoy this intriguing piece of genre history.

ABOUT THE AUTHOR

The sharp-eyed reader might have already noticed that no author is credited on this publication's cover. We can assure you that it's not due to some terrible oversight: we simply don't know with certainty who wrote the novella you are about to read.

The original Hungarian edition of *Dracula's Death* was released as issue six of a series of *Filmbooks*. The only credit within its pages belongs to Lajos Pánczél, as the series' editor. He was a prolific journalist and film critic, and he's the person most commonly accepted as the writer behind the book.

Further complicating things, when the book was cataloged at the National Széchényi Library (Hungary's national archives) in 1924, the film's writer-director, Károly Lajthay was entered into the records as the author. He was a well known filmmaker in his time, so we can speculate that the librarian making the entry simply wrote in the name they (and presumably the public in general) associated with the movie. Still, to this day, Lajthay is the author according to the library's database.

Even though Lajthay is the sole person credited with writing the screenplay for *Dracula's Death*, in a 1920 interview he stated that he co-wrote it with fellow filmmaker Mihály Kertész. Because of this, the novelization is sometimes attributed to both Lajthay *and* Kertész.

ABOUT THE ARTIST

József Sváb is a Hungarian comic book artist.

He is most known for illustrating stories in historical settings, such as his adaptations of works by Sir Arthur Conan Doyle, Oscar Wilde, and Max Brand. Sváb is also the writer of *Comics School*, the first guidebook in Hungary dedicated to the art of making comics, published in 1991. In 2018, he received the Pál Korcsmáros Award for his outstanding contribution to the medium.

His illustrations for *Dracula's Death* were created in 2020.

The cover of Drakula Halála (Dracula's Death), 1924

DRACULA'S DEATH

INTRODUCTION

This mystical tale transports us into the vivid realm of abounding human imagination. Into the stormy night of dreams and fantasy, where the quiet yet sinister comedy of frightening black shadows, the dying and the living-dead unfolds in a colorful mirage…

In the midst of this pitiful ensemble, like a lush oasis in a barren sand-desert, blooms a budding, beautiful creature: a young girl, whose frail spirit is taken by rampant madness… This weak soul is hopelessly chained to her fate, which thrusts her down the unforgiving waters of life, through menacing torrents, until finally the golden gates of happiness, joy and bright future open up in front of this much-tormented heroine of our drama…

In broad-strokes, this is the subject of this lively, captivating tale; the film version of which is truly the work of the Hungarian spirit.

Károly Lajthay wrote and directed this story, which is brought to the screen by the following cast:

DRACULA	Paul Askonas
MARY	Margit Lux
GEORGE	Dezső Kertész

The Chief Physician .... Elemér Thury
A Fake Surgeon .... Lajos Rethey
His Assistant .... Aladár Ihász
The Funny Lunatic .... Karl Götz

Further roles played by Lajos Szalkay, Károly Hatvani, Oszkár Perczel, Béla Timár, Paula Kende and Lene Myl.

I.
THE TRAGEDY OF OLD MR. LAND

Among the eternally snow-covered mountains of the Alpine lies a small village. Here, in this majestic silence, away from the racket of the world, alone lived little Mary Land, the poor seamstress. Her days were dreary and filled with sadness. She tried to ease her loneliness, her heart's everlasting sorrow with hard work. Day and night she worked tirelessly to earn her daily bread, and to support her sick father who was pining away at the city asylum.

In the poor little cottage, where Mary lived, the buzzing of the sewing machine never ceased, and her tired, frail fingers were always feverishly working.

Outside, as nature turned to winter, everything gleamed in God's eternal glory. The little village — surrounded by snowy mountains — lingered in an idyllic state, just like a tiny island in an endless sea. A deep silence settled on the village, where its peaceful residents — safely nestled in their humble homes — were resting after the year's hardship.

The small cottage that was Mary's home, and where she was born sixteen years before, was once a place of happiness. The girl's parents were well-off, and the family enjoyed a content, comfortable life… But one spring, shortly after Mary's mother fell ill, Death relieved her of her suffering just as suddenly. Old Mr. Land's sorrow was indescribable, and Mary's heart was bleeding for her late mother… This tragedy struck the girl's father with such might that he had lost his mind, and Mary, at the recommendation of his doctors, had him committed to the asylum in the capital city.

From here on, Mary lived alone in her house at the edge of the village. With growing strength and work ethic, she slaved away to support herself, and to provide for her father's treatment. Two dismal years passed like this… And even though Mary was worn out by the grueling work, her will didn't wane, as she would have given even her own life for her father. Sadly, two years of treatment didn't help old Mr. Land one bit. He withered away at the asylum, like a living corpse, and his doctors came to the conclusion — among themselves — that he was truly beyond help, that his days were numbered, and that a quick death would surely be mercy for such a miserable, lost man…

Mary visited her father weekly. That was the only time when Mr. Land's haunted eyes seemed to light up, emitting an otherwise dormant spark of life… Upon seeing his daughter, the old man would break into a kind of euphoria: he would kiss, hug and caress his only child, because secretly he knew that the end was near, and he would have to part with his only joy left on this Earth… Mary also understood that his father was saying goodbye; she tried to comfort her hopelessly sick father, but at the same time there were tears in her eyes too; yet she stayed quiet, and just endured the agonizing goodbye that neither of them wanted to acknowledge... They were deceiving each other... Their tearful glances were all lies, of a happier future and of the hope of a new life, even though they both heard a defeating, deathly "farewell" inside...

They both yearned for their weekly encounters, and at the end they parted broken, with an unshakable feeling in their hearts, as if they knew that the inevitable was near and that they might not see each other ever again...

II.
MARY AND GEORGE

Mary's only comfort in these torturous times was George Marlup, her fiance, who showered the blossoming girl — his one and only — with adoring love. George was a woodsman in the village over, and came daily to visit his fiance. The couple spent many idyllic hours together... During which the sadness fled Mary's heart: she shined, forgot about her endless sorrow, and she could finally envision her future... A bright, beautiful, happy future that would make up for the suffering of the past...

George treated Mary with warm love and tender attention. He tried to protect her from working so relentlessly: he warned her, caringly cautioned her to ease her heavy workload, which was taking a toll on the girl's frail nerves. But Mary was unyielding. She laboured endlessly, and even when George came over on the holy day of Christmas, he found her working.

"You stayed up all night again, my little Mary! Why can't you be kinder to yourself? After all, today is a holiday, the holy day of Christmas. I brought you this little tree. I will return this evening so we can decorate it together."

"My fate is to endure, and work" answered Mary with sadness "But I don't complain… I accepted the inevitable… I will keep carrying this burden…"

Tears were gleaming in Mary's sad eyes…

The young man set the small tree on the table, bestowed a warm kiss onto Mary's lips, and left.

"May God be with you, my Love" George said from the door, "Goodbye."

* * *

George returned to his fiance that night, and together they decorated the little Christmas tree, this beautiful, eternal symbol of love and peace… Then they prayed to the Heavenly Father with grateful hearts, and the ringing of the church bells outside intertwined with the words of their devotions, as the chapel down the village was calling for a midnight mass…

The small fir tree — this precious symbol of peace, now decorated with countless shiny ornaments and candles — cast a silvery glow on the two lovers… And now it seemed as if a halo surrounded Mary's golden-blond hair…

At this moment the couple was startled by a mysterious knock on the door. George opened it for the unexpected visitor, who turned out to be the local postman, delivering an urgent letter to Mary.

The girl nervously opened it:

To Miss Mary Land,

We regret to inform you that your father's condition has turned for the worst. It would be advisable to visit him as soon as possible.

Sincerely,
Capital City Mental Asylum
Dr. Faigner
Director and Chief Physician

Mary's eyes, which were gleaming with joy mere minutes ago, were now full of tears... Even though she knew, and was fully prepared for her father to not have much time left, the news still came as a shock, and she ran crying into George's arms. But then she suddenly looked up, and said:

"We can't miss the midnight mass! We have to hurry, George!"

The young man, without saying a word, took his fiance by the arm.

And as the bells of the little chapel rang through the valley, its devout residents were gathering for worship in the night...

Mary and George would not have missed the midnight mass. The girl and her fiancé said a heartfelt prayer to the Almighty, begging him to keep Mr. Land...

At the end of the service, Mary nervously turned to George:

"My dear, good father! Who knows if I'll find him alive? The next train doesn't come till the morning... and I'm afraid it might be too late by then!"

George felt the gravity of the situation, and tried to comfort his love:

"You can't waste a minute, Mary! I'll harness the horses and we'll leave immediately! We'll reach the city by dawn!"

He promptly turned his words into action. George readied the horses and the sleigh, and minutes later they were waiting in front of Mary's home, prepared for the journey.

The young man gently helped the heartbroken girl into the sleigh, as she was consumed by worry for his father's life.

The eager horses raced along with the couple. The little sleigh quickly slid on the frozen, snow-covered roads, and its jingling — like ethereal sound of silver bells — echoed through the dark night...

The journey took hours. Heavy, thick snow was falling from the skies...

It was past midnight. Mary — exhausted, and tormented by grief — drifted into sleep in the sleigh, as it was rushing her to the city far away, to her dying father...

* * *

The rising sun was sowing its first morning light when the young couple approached the city. In just a few minutes, they would reach the mental asylum.

It was morning… A crisp, fresh, clear winter morning. Still, the sun struggled to break through the foggy, cloudy air with its hot beam of light.

In front of the beautiful couple towered the somber, desolate building-giant: the madhouse.

Mary suddenly shivered.

"Oh!"

George rushed to the girl and embraced her before she could faint:

"My Dear, what happened? What is wrong?"

"It's always like this. It happens every time I arrive at this building, and think that my poor, good father lives here, senseless and his life empty! Oh, this is a terrible fate, George! This house is the realm of the living-dead,

only the most unfortunate people live here, and among them is my dear father! But I still remember him! His kind face, his gentle eyes, the endless love that he always surrounded me with. He raised me with so, so much love — yet, this is where he is now. Is this where man's journey must end?!"

George tried to comfort her with these gentle words:

"Be calm, my dear! We cannot know the path of fate, and we must take solace in God's will, even when it is trying for us! You must be brave now! I believe that you will find your poor father alive, and even that shall bring you some comfort."

Upon hearing George's words, Mary calmed down somewhat. They arrived at the gates of the madhouse.

Mary spoke before entering:

"Thank you for accompanying me, George. I will return with the night train. Farewell, my Love!"

They parted with a warm kiss goodbye.

"Don't delay, Mary" said George to his fiance, "May God be with you! Farewell!"

The girl entered this house of sorrow.

She walked down the corridor with hesitant, nervous steps: her heart was somber, and she was trembling with fear for her father's life.

She approached the first person she saw:

"Excuse me, may I speak with Doctor Tillner?"

She barely finished her question when Doctor Tillner appeared in front of her. He was one of the chief physicians of the hospital. He was wearing a white coat, as he was getting ready for his morning rounds.

Mary knew Doctor Tillner well, whose ward her father was on; she met with him every time she visited.

"What happened to my father? Is he alive? Don't spare me, doctor, just tell me the truth!"

With wide eyes and a cracking voice, Mary put her questions to the doctor, who listened to her for a little while, and then tried to calm his dismayed visitor with these somber words:

"Take comfort, young lady! Death can only be salvation for your poor father. Come with me and look around among my patients: what miserable lives these human wrecks live here!"

III.
SHADOW PEOPLE

Mary followed the doctor with intrigue. Doctor Tillner led her towards the hospital's garden.

All the asylum's residents were already outside. Instinctively they yearned to be outside on this sunny winter morning, which had a calming effect on their dead nerves and crippled spirits. Upon seeing the girl and the doctor, the legion of patients — as if part of a colorful panopticon — all started to stare — with their confused, query eyes — at Mary, the unexpected visitor.

The girl nervously stayed by Doctor Tillner's side, because even though she knew some of the patients from her many visits to her father, seeing them all together, in a crowd, was a strange and miserable sight that startled her.

Her fear intensified as they started to slowly move closer to her. There was a demented, frightening glow in their eyes. Warily, as if they were seeing a foe in Mary, they seemed ready to attack her, and they slowly dragged their broken, tired, wrecked bodies towards her…

Doctor Tiller, seeing what was happening, motioned towards the patients, who scattered into retreat, but with eyes still glowing with spiteful hatred.

"Don't be afraid, my child," said Doctor Tillner encouragingly "They're all harmless, couldn't even hurt a fly. Only their appearance seems dangerous. I could even say that they're cowardly, who would easily be frightened by the rustle of a leaf."

The chief physician, in order to disperse the girl's unfounded fear — after all, these poor souls, despite their menacing behaviour, were harmless — started to head back to the building as they talked.

"This one," he said, "is a famous scientist, who believes that his legs are made of glass, and would break if he took one single step."

Doctor Tiller pointed towards a large man sitting under a tree, with his legs tightly wrapped in towels and blankets.

"And that one, over there, believes himself to be the Secretary of the Treasury. He keeps handing out checks for billions to his fellow inmates."

Mary saw a lanky, thin man wearing an outrageous outfit: he was frantically writing into a notebook, and tearing the pages out just so he can quickly give them to the other patients. His scrawny, pale face lit up with pure joy as he did that.

The chief physician was ready to finish their talk when a tall, lean man with matted hair and the face of Beelzebub caught Mary's eye.

"Who is that frightening man? He's looking at me the way a murderer must look at his victim. He's devouring me with his eyes, which seem to glow with all the colors of Hell."

"He used to be a distinguished composer." answered Doctor Tillner "But now he believes himself to be a monarch. He won't part with his royal cloak even at night."

"Interesting! He looks just like the organ player who taught me to sing many years ago at the orphanage." said Mary.

"If you're not too afraid, you should speak to him." said the chief physician "No matter what I ask, he won't answer me."

IV.
DRACULA

Mary, at the encouragement of the chief physician, approached the man in the royal cloak, who was now staring at her with an eerie grin. She was getting somewhat comfortable with this strange group of unusual people, so she dared to speak to him:

"How are you, Sir? Do you remember me? My name is Mary Land… Five years ago, at the orphanage…"

"I don't remember." said the terrifying figure "I don't remember anything! I am Dracula… The Immortal!"

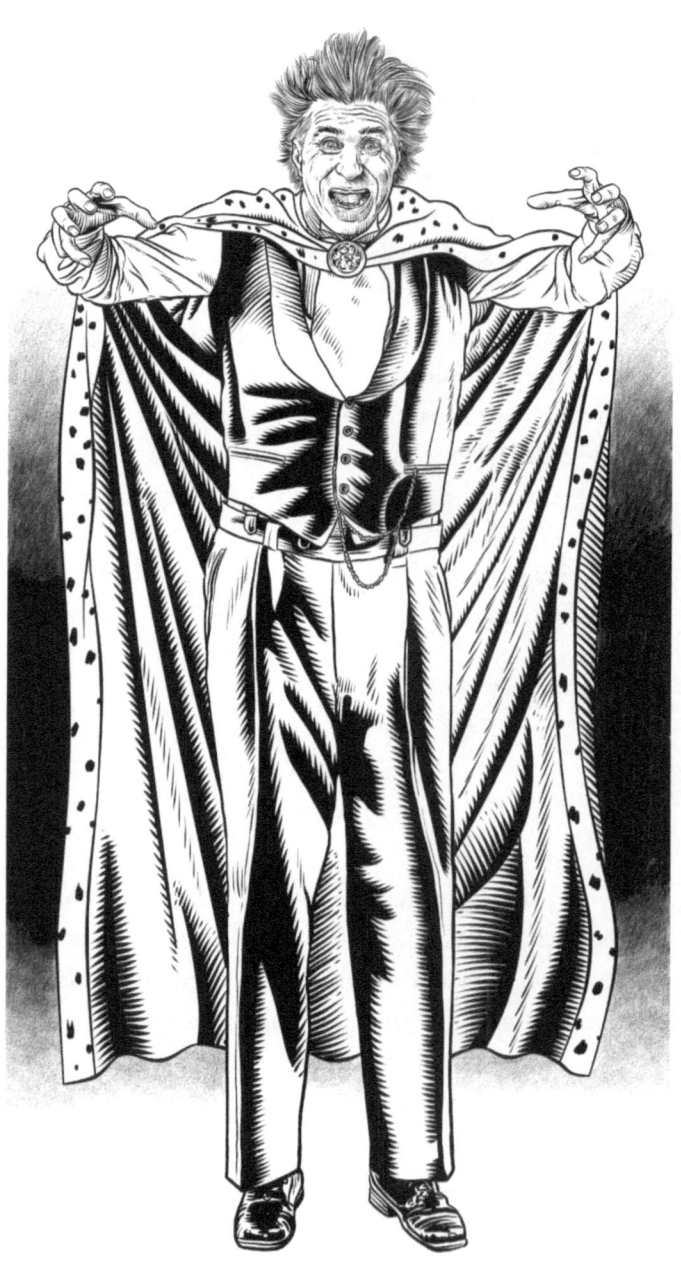

An untamed fire was burning in the man's heart. And in a wild, jarring voice he shouted again:

"Yes! I am Dracula... The Immortal!"

Mary Land got shivers upon seeing the frightening figure. She regretted initiating the conversation, but upon recalling the doctor's reassuring words, she continued:

"Remember back, Sir... I was there, in the second row... I sang soprano, and you used to pat me on the head in approval... a long time ago... but I can still remember everything."

The madman shuddered:

"I've lived for a thousand years and I will live forever... Immortality is mine... Immortality! I am eternal... Men die, the world can crumble, but I will live, live forever!"

Mary slowly backed away from Dracula, who continued:

"My life is eternal. Death will never come for me! Oh, — don't think that I am mad, too! I am only here because I love these living-dead; I truly pity them and I want to give them their lives back!"

Mary listened to Dracula, this man-like monster, whose voice was like a roaring rumble from Hell, and whose deep-seated eyes were gleaming with black flames. He towered over the frail woman as if he were to squeeze the life out of her with one single embrace.

Doctor Tillner, who was watching the scene unfold from afar, hurried up to the girl and escorted her back to the hospital. He led her into an operating room, where he said:

"Please take a seat here while I speak to the Director, and ask him to provide a private room for your father."

"I was truly frightened by that man with the matted hair… Dracula." she said with a trembling voice.

"Stay strong." said the chief physician "Dracula is only frightening in appearance. There's no need to be afraid of him. Please calm down."

Mary sat down nervously in the sparkling white operating room. She was still shaking. Her encounter with Dracula, like a heavy, insuppressible memory, kept repeating in her mind. And as she was sitting there, lost in her thoughts, the door suddenly swung open, and a surgeon-like figure in a white coat entered.

Mary gripped the chair she was sitting on. She was terrified of this stranger, who might have looked like a doctor, but who struck fear in her with his sinister gaze.

He was one of the patients. A lean figure, with a bony, stiff face, who was staring at the frightened girl with cloudy eyes. This madman thought himself to be a surgeon, and was constantly wearing a doctor's coat. He went around examining his fellow inmates with boastful coldness, and he was always eager to operate on them.

"I am Professor Wells" he said to Mary "A doctor of medical science! If you don't mind, young lady, I'm going to take a look at you."

And with that he sat down next to Mary, and started examining her.

V.
THE TWO DOCTORS

Mary had no idea that the person inspecting her was a madman hiding behind the mask of a doctor, but her instincts told her that she was in danger. She feared, even dreaded this ominous man who kept staring at her.

"Please tell me: do your eyes hurt?" he suddenly broke the silence, and started inspecting the girl's eyes.

"My diagnosis is sound! You suffer from serious eye trouble, Miss!" the fake doctor continued, "If you don't undergo immediate surgery, you will surely lose your sight!"

Mary was stunned by this new revelation. Her doubts about the man vanished: she believed him, and was now convinced that he was indeed a doctor.

At this moment the door opened again, and another man wearing a white coat entered. Professor Wells' face lit up, and he said to Mary:

"If you don't believe me, just ask my colleague." he gestured towards the other man.

The second fake doctor looked at Mary's eyes with great curiosity, and then proclaimed his diagnosis:

"Vulpis Doloris! To be operated on immediately!"

Mary tried to pull herself away from the two men in terror, but they grabbed her and forced her onto the operating table. They strapped her arms and legs down. Professor Wells took a long surgical knife out of a cabinet and approached the terrified girl.

This all unfolded in just a few quick moments.

A shriek broke through Mary's throat:

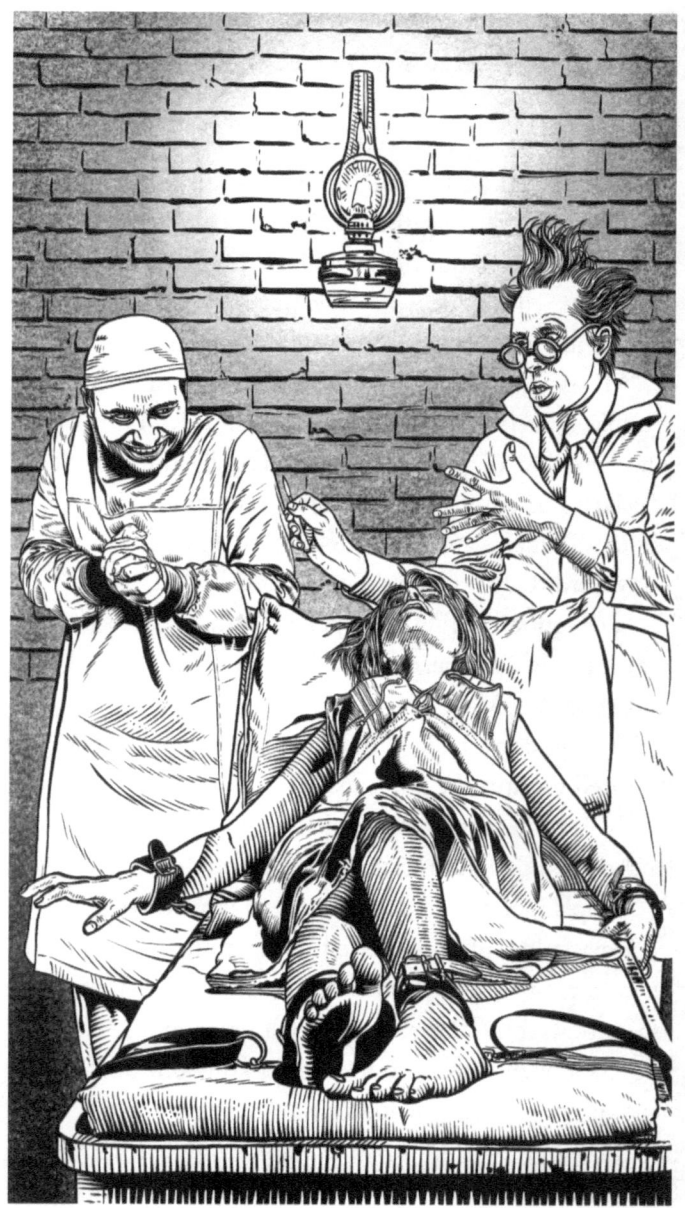

"For God's sake… Let me go…! Help!"

"Stay still!" yelled one of the fake surgeons to the struggling girl.

"Be grateful that we're performing the operation!" said the other lunatic "You will owe us your life, your eyesight…! We'll be done in no time!"

Mary screamed:

"No. I won't let you! Let me go! Thank you, but let me go!"

The two madmen — with crazed eyes — launched themselves at the girl, who was now fighting back with all her strength. She tried to tear herself away from the operating table, and she kept shouting as she struggled desperately:

"Help! Help me!"

Her cries echoed off the white walls, and it seemed that she might meet a cruel, grotesque fate in this terrible place.

Like a bird in a cast net, she struggled in the arms of the two madmen. Then Mary suddenly fell quiet, and a heavy, devastating silence engulfed the room.

The two lunatics were about to pierce through the struggling girl's eyes when finally her cries for help were answered: a couple of nurses and Doctor Tillner himself charged into the room, overpowered the madmen and freed the girl from the straps.

Mary lay there, broken and swooned… Took her an hour to regain herself and her strength.

Doctor Tillner watched over her, observed her labored breathing, her restless body, which was still greatly affected by the horrific event.

The girl finally opened her eyes.

"What happened to me?" she asked in a frightened voice "Was it maybe a dream? Was I struck by a wicked nightmare…? Or have I really lived through such terrible things?"

The chief physician tried to comfort the trembling girl with fatherly warmth.

"Everything will be alright, little Mary." he said "Forget what happened, think of it as nothing but a bad dream."

Oh, it was dreadful just to think about!

It was careless for her to be alone here, although no one suspected that she would have such deranged visitors.

Mary wiped her forehead, as if she could shoo away the wicked memories, and then, with Doctor Tillner's help, she left the operating room.

Mary now went to see her father, who was in his final moments. The dying man tightly embraced his daughter. Mary's tears washed down old Mr. Land's face… And then he gave a loud grunt… the sick man's reaching hand gave away… his boney fingers stiffened… his head fell to the side… and he closed his cloudy eyes one final time…

Mary collapsed onto her father's lifeless corpse, crying. Doctor Tillner carried the broken-hearted, distressed girl out of the room, who was so struck by these strange events that she wasn't sure whether they had really happened, or were they simply all a nightmare.

The chief physician dragged the fainting girl to the room next to the director's office, where he put her on the couch so she could compose herself. But Mary wanted to leave. She wanted to run, escape from this wicked house, where she had been so tormented; this place, where the most dreadful memories of her life were bound to.

"I… I want to go… to get away… My life is in grave danger here! Let me leave!" screamed the overwrought girl.

Doctor Tiller could barely restrain her.

"You can't go anywhere in such a hysterical state!" he said, "Stay for the night and rest. You'll feel better by morning and then you can travel home!"

Mary finally gave in to the reassuring words of the doctor. She laid down on the couch, and soon thereafter she fell into a deep sleep.

"I'm begging you… don't hurt me… I don't deserve it." she murmured as she drifted into a dream, and then she fell quiet.

VI.
DRACULA'S ASSAULT

She slept for hours… And when the clock in the tower struck midnight, Dracula, like an unholy phantom, appeared in her room. He silently moved toward the sleeping girl, and touched her shoulder with his long, boney fingers, which startled her awake. Stunned, Mary looked up at Dracula, whose eyes were gleaming with terrifying visions of Hell. A diabolical grin marred his lips, and as if he was about to launch himself at his victim, he embraced the girl and started to drag her out of the room:

"Come with me!" he said "We're going to my castle, to the palace of pleasures! I want to save you! These people here are all evil, who want to destroy you — just like they did with your father!"

Mary listened to this earthy devil in fear, and Dracula, with great self-assurance, continued:

"You have to escape this Hell! Trust in me and do as I say! I am immortal and I possess otherworldly powers! Come!"

"No! In God's name, let me go!" Mary objected, "Who are you...? What do you want from me...? By what right do you demand that I go with you?! Where are you taking me?"

Dracula, like a storm, carried his victim, dragged her and pulled her, so they could reach their destination before dawn...

Outside, a mysterious veil of darkness engulfed the city... Thick, heavy snow was falling from the sky, and it turned the landscape into dreadful black-and-white...

The human monster hauled the frightened girl outside, as if she was a helpless ragdoll, and she had no choice but to follow him... They roamed desperately for hours, until they arrived at a towering, mysterious building, Dracula's castle.

Mary trembled.

The chilling cold wind made her shiver, and she was appalled by her strange companion. She tried to tear herself away from Dracula, but the monster had a strong grip on her.

"Haha! My Darling!" he laughed with his devilish voice "Joy, happiness and pleasure await you here! Why would you want to get away?!"

"Let me go! Let me go!"

"You will now enter the realm of immortality, the palace of wonders: Dracula's house! Do not be afraid, and do not fret! You should rejoice, because happiness awaits you! Come, come!"

The girl's resistance was futile. Their struggle was unequal, and Dracula prevailed...

The wings of the immense stone gate parted in front of them with a loud creak. Dracula had arrived home with his prey.

Once inside, Mary looked around with frightened curiosity: the palace — with its strange architecture, and fantastical lighting — reminded her of the enchanted kingdoms of fairy tales.

A strange, intoxicating odor lingered in Dracula's castle. This heavy, suffocating smell almost stunned the frail-minded girl.

"Why did you bring me here?...!" Mary finally asked "What do you want with me?"

Dracula replied triumphantly:

"You can never escape this place! Tomorrow we'll celebrate our engagement! You will become my bride! I will mark you with an eternal kiss and you will stay here among my immortal wives."

With that, Dracula waved his hand, and the marble floor opened up in the middle of the palace. Blue and violet lights came up from below… Unearthly music seeped through… and twelve beautiful women appeared: their youthful bodies were only covered by delicate veils, and they were dancing to the warm rhythm…

Dracula broke Mary's silence:

"By the second sunrise, you will be one of my subterranean residents!"

"No… I wouldn't want to get down there for all the treasures of the world!" cired Mary, and in desperation she grabbed the cross hanging around her neck, and started praying to God to save her from this wicked place.

"Damnation! Hell…! The only thing I'm powerless against… Away with it!" shouted Dracula.

VII.
THE WEDDING

The first warm lights of the morning sun flooded the castle.

Dracula yelled as he was fleeing:

"I despise the daylight! It repulses me! Farewell — good night!"

Dracula left, and the gates of the castle all closed.

Mary was left alone in the mysterious building, but she imagined seeing Dracula's menacing figure on every corner… She tried to escape this phantom, but to no avail… the image of Dracula followed her everywhere.

Dismal hours passed like this. Mary hopelessly wandered the halls of her prison, from which escaping was a mere daydream... She dragged her shivering body from one room to the next, looking for a way out — in vain... And the terrifying vision — Dracula's menacing grin — only fueled her fear and desperation...

Dusk was soon upon her... She ran out to the palace's garden, when the majestic gate slowly opened and Dracula entered...

"How kind of you to come out to greet me!" he said to the startled girl.

Then he grabbed her by the arm and led her back into the castle.

"Now go and get ready for our engagement ceremony!"

Dracula gestured to his enslaved wives, who surrounded Mary and led her into a perfumed, flowery room. A wedding dress — adorned with gold, silver, and precious stones — was prepared for her. The wives put her in the lavish gown, and when Dracula's newest bride was ready, they led her down to the great hall of the palace, where the devil's son was already waiting for her.

Dracula rushed to his bride with a luscious grin. Mary — in a state of swoon — gave herself away to the wicked man's will.

"I bid you welcome, my beautiful bride!" Dracula flattered Mary "We are here to celebrate a joyful occasion, the eve of our nuptials!"

Shrill music soared... a wicked wedding-march: harsh, twisted and strange music, to which costumed ballerinas performed a sensual dance...

The entire palace was engulfed in mystical lights… Blinding colors intertwined… A vivid flash of light erupted, then died down, just to be followed by another one.

This was an extravagant and eerie celebration, Dracula's engagement, where he was to make his newest bride his prisoner.

"After the flowers rain, my kiss will unite us for an eternity!" said the groom.

Following his words, like a summer shower, thousands of flowers fell from the ceiling, covering everything…

A seductive scent filled up the large room…

Dracula turned to Mary with lustful eyes, eager to kiss the girl… His lips were trembling with desire, and his arms were about to embrace her. At this moment Mary understood the grave danger she was in, so she pushed Dracula away, reached for the cross hanging around her neck and held it up for him to see…

"The cross…! The cross…!" Dracula shrieked as he backed away from the girl.

Witnessing this unexpected sight, terror spread quickly through the entire room… All the evil spirits scattered away along with Dracula…

There was now an open path for Mary…

And the girl, taking advantage of this opportunity, started to run, through the gate that was left wide open, and into the snowy night.

VIII.
DOWN THE PATH OF DEATH

She just ran, and ran, to escape from this Palace of Hell, and from Dracula; but she couldn't keep dragging her exhausted body for too long... She collapsed on the snow-covered ground, under a tree, where she lay till dawn...

She was found in the morning by people who came upon her by chance. She was still lying on the icy ground, unconscious.

A kind family took Mary back to their house, but she didn't regain herself, even after long hours had passed.

They tried everything to revive her, but their efforts were to no avail.

Mary Land was still unconscious, yet in her head, her delirium culminated in an agonizing St Vitus' dance.

She was tormented by wicked, evil visions.

She kept seeing Dracula's unholy grin, his piercing eyes, his wicked features... and his hands that were so eager to strangle!

"No... no... don't hurt me..." she uttered occasionally through her bone-dry lips.

Mary's rescuers watched over the poor girl with great compassion.

"We have to call for a doctor!" said the head of the household "We won't know anything about her until she regains herself! Who knows what secrets she hides?"

His younger brother immediately started preparing to journey into the city for a doctor.

Meanwhile, Mary's agony wouldn't ease. She was still tormented by fever-dreams that threatened to destroy her.

They put cold snow on her forehead and her burning face, in an effort to try to relieve her fever.

Outside, the jingling of the sleigh faded into the distance: the boy was on his way to the city to get help.

A deep silence fell on the little room: only Mary's labored breathing could be heard.

And then, the door suddenly swung open.

Mary's rescuers were stunned when they saw the unexpected dark figure: Dracula. The devilish creature frightened these simple people.

The howling wind blew snow into the room.

Dracula entered the room without a word, closed the door behind himself, and approached Mary's bed.

He paid no heed to the family watching him in disbelief.

"I am here because there's a need for a doctor: the rest doesn't matter!" he said to them.

"But who sent for you?" asked the head of the household "How did you get here? My brother only now left for the city."

Dracula, without ever acknowledging the question, walked up to the still unconscious girl, and examined her:

"She is a lunatic, and must have escaped from one of the asylums! She has to be removed from here promptly, because she could very well be dangerous!"

Those around him were enchanted by Dracula's powerful words.

Uncomfortable silence set in…

Dracula seemed to have hypnotized the household with his dazzling eyes, and they all just stood there, silently, and allowed this strange, terrifying figure to do as he pleased.

And he never took his glimmering, wild eyes off the girl in the bed, who'd been becoming more and more restless ever since he arrived.

"Don't forsake me! Save me! Help…! He's going to kill me!" she screamed in visceral terror.

Hearing this, the evil grin deepened on Dracula's cruel face.

He stood next to the girl's bed with his arms crossed, as the house's frightened residents stared at him in silence.

In the meanwhile, the city doctor arrived, who was brought here by the patriarch's brother.

"The doctor found the girl to be a dangerous lunatic!" explained the head of the household to the newly arrived doctor, who now took a closer look at Mary and Dracula.

"I'm afraid my colleague here is mistaken. I see wounds, and high fever…"

And he continued:

"This seems to be a rather unusual case. I will stay here so I can make accurate observations."

Dracula, upon hearing the real doctor's words, suddenly disappeared.

* * *

Days passed since then… Mary was struggling to overcome her illness, but in a week she was back to feeling cheerful again, as if she had forgotten the sorrowful events that transpired. And truth be told, Mary didn't really remember what had happened. She just felt as if she had woken up from a terrible fever-dream, from a long, torturous nightmare. No matter how much the family — that so kindly took her in and cared for her as one of their very own — asked, she couldn't give them answers.

One day, after examining the girl, the doctor gladly declared:

"Mary is on her way to recovery! Soon she will be healthy again, and then she can finally marry her fiance!"

IX.
A RUTHLESS NIGHT

One night, when the entire group was together, a footman arrived at the house.

"The doctor is needed!" he said to the physician "Somebody got injured at the sports field! They're waiting for you!"

"Who are you?" asked the doctor.

"I'm a carrier!" said the peasant-looking man "I take hotel guests to the train station and back."

"But it's pitch black outside!" noted the doctor with great concern.

"You have nothing to be afraid of, doctor! I know these roads very well, and my horse is reliable." the carrier assured him.

The doctor was overtaken by his sense of duty, so he agreed to leave with the carrier.

He said goodbye to Mary and the others, and promised to promptly return once he finished with the visit.

Outside, the night was dark, and dense fog blanketed the landscape.

The snow creaked under their steps.

The physician set down in the sleigh, the carrier took his place on the box seat, picked up the reins, and the wooden hull was underway.

The doctor looked back. The bright window of the warm house slowly faded into the distance. The sleigh was quickly sliding away on the white snow.

The carrier drove faster and faster. The sleigh was just about flying through the air. The road was invisible in front of them: the pitch dark night and the heavy fog enshrouded everything.

On the monotone journey through the dark night, in the burning light of his cigar, the good doctor thought of Mary, and he felt grateful that he could nurse this kind, happy, blossoming girl back to life.

The sleigh was flying, even faster than before, and the only liveliness in the foggy and mysterious night was the jingling of the horses' bells…

After about a quarter of an hour, the doctor voiced his concern to the carrier:

"Where exactly are you taking me?"

The carrier either didn't hear his question, or chose to ignore it, because he just continued to ride the horses.

The doctor was astonished, and asked again, even louder this time:

"Where are we going…? Where are you taking me?! — Stop the sleigh!"

But his voice got lost in the night. The doctor checked his pockets, but he didn't have any weapons on him. He could see that the carrier was taking him off the familiar roads, and he now suspected that a ruthless plan was behind his silence.

Yet, he didn't lose heart.

Carried away by the sense of danger and suspense, the doctor repeated his question:

"Tell me, at last, where you're taking me! Where are we going?" asked the distraught passenger.

This is when the sleigh entered a hazardous mountain path that ran alongside a terribly deep abyss… It would have only taken a small slip, and the wooden sleigh, along with its passengers, would have fallen into it…

Even the carrier recognized the grave danger, so he finally admitted:

"A mysterious man in black gave me a gold coin and ordered me to bring you here, doctor!"

"You fool!" shouted the doctor "Turn around at once! Our lives are at stake!"

In this critical moment, the doctor's dire warning seemed effective. The carrier, who was bribed by Dracula himself, carefully turned the sleigh around and took his passenger back to the kind family's house.

On the way back, the doctor questioned the carrier, who was only able to give a vague description of the dishonest man who had paid him off. But even this was enough for the doctor to realize that the person who had bribed the carrier was in fact the mysterious, strange man he first met by Mary's sick bed.

The doctor knew that this enigmatic person must have been an enemy of Mary's, this innocent, hapless girl. He tried to send her to a mental asylum as a means to kidnap her. And proof of his hatred for the girl was that he was even willing to endanger the life of a doctor fulfilling his duty.

But this realization was all in vain, since he couldn't do anything about this mysterious foe, as the doctor didn't know where he lived.

Meanwhile, the house where the family cared for Mary was enshrined in a deep silence. Everyone was asleep, and only Mary was tormented by unsettling dreams... And right around midnight she was startled awake by a strange sound... As if she heard the muffled, otherworldly screech of an owl... Her entire body shivered... She looked around in the darkness... Her eyes turned towards the dim lamp... looking for the source of mysterious sound, but she found nothing.

She fell back into her bed, and tried to go back to sleep.

Outside, the icy wind was roaring viciously. She could not close her eyes. The flickering lamp cast a mysterious gloom on the room, and Mary thought that she was seeing colorful shadows on the white walls.

And then she remembered Dracula...

The good doctor and the nurturing environment made her forget about the horrors that had transpired. The terrifying memory was dissolving in her mind, but on this strange night it all flared right back up.

"Hoo-hoo-hoooo…" Mary couldn't tell if she was really hearing an owl, or if it was just her imagination…

Then the dusky shadows started to grow and swirl in front of her very eyes.

Sweat rolled down her forehead, and her body was burning with blazing fever.

She tossed and turned in terror. She tried to forget the past, she shut her eyes in a mulish attempt, buried her head in her pillow, as she just wanted to sleep, nothing but to sleep.

She murmured old prayers that promised to bring her deep and reassuring dreams.

But she couldn't keep her eyes closed: to the contrary, pain pierced through her eyelids, and no matter how much Mary tried to withstand it, she had to keep them open.

"God... Please don't forsake me!" she begged in a soft voice, because she felt that her life was at a terrible crossroads.

The wind outside was blowing more and more viciously; it rattled the window and Mary thought that a thousand screams were echoing in its loud roar.

Horrible minutes passed like this, and each felt like long, grim hours to the frightened girl...

And as Mary glanced at the glimmering lamp, she saw it fall down with a loud thud: flames followed in its wake, which quickly spread out onto the carpet, until the entire room was ablaze... Mary jumped out of her bed and ran from the all-consuming fire... out into the cold winter night...

And as if something was after her, she kept running into the white night... She couldn't feel the cold of the snow, or the icy wind, she just kept running, running away...

X.
THE DEVIL FLEW AWAY

And this is where the terrifying dream ended...
Mary woke up, and looked around the operating room with fright in her eyes: its snowwhite furnishing — and the operating table that invoked death itself — scared the girl, who just rose from a truly dreadful nightmare...

Outside, the red morning sun was shining... Nature was waking, and so was the hospital with its pitiful residents...

Mary looked around the room, still confused. She slowly raised her hand and touched her forehead.

She thought back of the ruthless night, and her soul, as if it just escaped from a dreadful vision, was elated that it was all just a dream.

And then she got somber again when a terrible thought crossed her mind. So many strange things have happened to her since she arrived at this wretched place.

The incident in the operating room; the all too real nightmare. Her nerves were trembling and her heart was pounding in her chest.

Mary thought of her father, crazy, old Mr. Land, and that's when she heard the erratic clamor of the lunatics coming from the garden.

"Maybe… maybe… Am I, too?.." as the thought crossed Mary's mind, she started shivering as if icy hands were touching her.

Now the operating room's door opened, but Mary didn't even have the strength to look up…

* * *

Doctor Tillner's first stop during his morning rounds took him to the operating room. Mary was lying on the couch, with her eyes open: she was wide awake, but she didn't have the energy yet to get up. A nurse stood next to her, and she was the one that the doctor addressed.

"The poor creature must have had a bad dream! She was screaming all night." answered the nurse.

Doctor Tillner gently drew the girl closer to himself; she was still scared, shaking, and she kept looking around the room still expecting to see that wicked Dracula…

"What is… what happened to me?!" she asked the chief physician "Am I awake…? Or is this still part of the terrifying dream?"

"Calm down, my dear." Doctor Tillner said to the girl "It was only a dream — Forget all about it!"

XI.
DRACULA'S DEATH

The patients were gathering in the mental asylum's garden. The strange ensemble continued its familiar comedy: the scientist was guarding his "glass legs", the "Secretary of Treasury" was handing out checks; and Dracula, the former composer, was preaching to his fellow inmates about his immortality. They seemed to be tired of it, and giggled at the man and his unusual delusions.

Among these living-dead was a rather tubby man, who wore a long, pointed top hat on his giant head. A large pair of ocular lenses sat on his thick nose. He had a permanent, grotesque grin on his face, and he was constantly playing jokes on his mates. With time, they all got used to his childish banter.

This morning, the "Funny Man" — because this is what the other inmates called him — somehow got his hands on a loaded revolver, and went on to terrorize the others with it. And even though they didn't think that it was loaded, they ran from the "Funny Man".

The armed lunatic then got in front of Dracula, aimed his gun at him and broke into a twisted laughter.

Dracula almost screamed with joy, and said this to the "Funny Man":

"At last I can prove that I'm immortal! Shoot!"

His voice boomed through every corner of the garden, and all the inmates rushed towards Dracula and the "Funny Man".

Dracula kept shouting:

"Don't hesitate, you cowardly bastard! You always blatantly stare at me, never believing in my immortality, so come closer, gather around, to look and marvel! The bullet will bounce off of Dracula — because Dracula is immortal! Ha-ha-haha! So come… here, here… all… all of you! And you… Raise your revolver!"

The "Funny Man" started to nervously back away from Dracula.

"No… I don't dare do it… I'm afraid." he said, and he slowly lowered the revolver.

"You aren't scared, are you? Coward! Shoot, I command you! Here… in my chest!" Dracula shouted at the "Funny Man".

The frightened group that gathered around the two madmen was getting more and more intrigued by the scene unfolding.

And the "Funny Man", obeying the order, cocked the revolver and pulled the trigger…

The bullet went straight through Dracula's heart and killed him.

His blood left a red stain on the fresh snow.

The inmates scattered away in fear at the sound of the gunfire, and the next minute Doctor Tillner and the nurses surrounded Dracula's body.

"Dracula's dead!" said one of the nurses to the doctor "The "Funny Man" shot him with a stolen revolver!"

The murderous lunatic, seeing the terrible consequences of his actions, was scared at first, but soon he began to laugh again. His face was distorted by his manic howling, as he calmly allowed the nurses to restrain him and take him away to his cell.

XII.
DOWN THE ROAD OF LOVE

A jinging sledge stopped in front of the madhouse. George — Mary's fiance — got out. The young man, after waiting up for his bride to no avail the night before, feared the worst, so he came to the city to find out what had happened, and to take the girl home.

Mary, upon seeing George, ran into his arms, and the lovers shared a long, happy kiss...

"Thank God!" rejoiced the young man "That I see you at last... I was so worried... afraid that something happened to you...! But tell me, why didn't you return last night? What kept you here?"

A flood of questions poured out of George's mouth, but Mary didn't have the patience nor the time to answer, because Doctor Tillner approached them. The couple said goodbye to the chief physician, and they were leaving the hospital through the garden. As they walked, arm in arm, two nurses carried Dracula — who met his tragic end — on a stretcher. Mary, as the somber procession passed them, caught a glance of Dracula's terrifying face, which was even more frightening now than when he was alive. She fearfully pulled closer to George, who — even though he still hadn't learned about his fiance's nightmare — drew her to himself.

They carried Dracula away...

A notebook fell out of the dead man's pocket. George picked it up and looked at its cover:

DIARY OF

MY IMMORTAL LIFE

AND ADVENTURES

Dracula

Mary also glanced at the book, and with a frightened voice she demanded:

"Drop it immediately! I don't want to see it! This man was the cause of my dreadful nightmares!"

George did as his bride asked. He threw away the notebook, put his arm around Mary, and helped her into the sledge...

The wooden hull left with a merry jingle, taking the lovers back, towards their home and happiness...

On the way George tried to get his quiet fiance to talk. But Mary's lips stayed silent. She wouldn't reveal even a word about her tormented dream. George never learned her secret.

The young man eased up on the questions. His unwaveringly silent bride never spoke about that night ever again…

THE END

THE DEVIL FLEW AWAY

THE HISTORY OF DRACULA'S DEATH
By László Tamásfi

Talking about the silent film era is talking about movies that we can't see today.

The Library of Congress estimates that as much as 75% of the films made before 1929 are lost, and that is just in the United States. This percentage is even higher in some other countries; in Hungary — for example — it's about 93%. This is a devastating statistic, especially if we consider how important the time period was for the art form. This is when the language of filmmaking was invented. Movies began as short slice-of-life scenes where the spectacle was still the "moving picture" itself, and evolved into narrative works that are very much like our modern films. Everything had to be invented, from screenwriting, cinematography, special effects, editing, all the way to distribution and exhibition, and it all happened in the silent era.

There are, of course, a lot of notable films that survived. Even just within the horror genre, we are very fortunate that we can watch John Barrymore's Dr. Jekyll turn into Mr. Hyde, we can visit Dr. Caligari at the fair, explore the futuristic cityscape of Metropolis, feel terror as Count

Orlok rises from his coffin, and see the Golem come to life in front of our very eyes.

But for every classic that survived, there are dozens that didn't. We'll never see the silver screen's first werewolf, the first Dracula, first Dr. Jekyll, or the first Phantom, and we will never get to watch Lon Chaney's vampire in what is arguably the most famous lost film in history, *London After Midnight*.

Still, in a way, even these movies are survivors. The sad reality is that most films from this time period are not only lost, but they're also completely *forgotten*. They were made, shown in theaters, some were hits with audiences and some flopped, some were praised by critics while others were certainly panned, but today, a hundred years later, nobody remembers them either way. We don't know their titles, or what they were about. No one is digging through archives looking for them.

In this regard, *Dracula's Death* is one of the lucky ones. It's the subject of quite a lot of attention, undoubtedly because it marked the first on-screen appearance of Count Dracula, just one year prior to F. W. Murnau's *Nosferatu*. It was made by noted filmmakers, and the press was paying attention to it, at least in its native Hungary. While it's true that we can't see the film as it was intended, if we string together the surviving articles, production photos, advertisements, and even a prose adaptation, we can map the history of the film's development and release... And if we squint our eyes just enough, we might even get a glimpse of a Dracula that hasn't been seen for almost a century.

Károly Lajthay (1883-1946) was already an established director when he set out to make *Dracula's Death*. He was born in the town of Marosvásárhely, and began his career as a stage actor, working for several theater companies across the Hungarian side of the Austro-Hungarian Empire before settling in Budapest. This is where he was introduced to the film industry,

Károly Lajthay

first as an actor, and shortly thereafter as a writer and director. He played roles in movies such as *Saint Peter's Umbrella* (1917), *The Rich Poors* (1917), and *The Severed Hand* (1920). His writing credits include *Crime and Punishment* (1917), and *Cursed Castle* (1918), but he spent the majority of his career in the director's chair, helming over a dozen movies between 1918 and 1944. He founded his own production company, Rex Film, in 1917. Like many of his peers in the early 1920's, he moved to Austria in order to find work, which is the context of the earliest surviving report of *Dracula's Death*, in an article published in *Szinházi Élet (Theater Life)* on December 26, 1920:

HUNGARIAN DIRECTORS IN VIENNA

Vienna can't seem to get by without Hungarian directors these days: at first Mihály Kertész, and then Sándor Korda was lured away by Vienna's biggest studio: the Sascha. They were followed by Szőreghy. And now Károly Lajthay defected to Vienna where he's been making movies for a long time. Károly Lajthay is back in Pest now, where he's negotiating with the Corvin film studio about renting studio space. He said the following to "Szinházi Élet" about filmmaking in Vienna:

"The movie business in Vienna is practically in Hungarian hands, as Hungarian directors dominate here. Korda and Kertész have unprecedented success.

The Sándor Korda-directed The Prince and the Pauper has made it to Pest since. You have seen it at its press-screening and must have recognized that it's simply perfect. Now Kertész completed his latest movie, it's called "Cherchez la femme." It already had its in-house premiere in front of an invited audience. Those who were lucky enough to be present all came away gushing about Kertész's latest masterpiece. The leading female role is once again played by Lucy Doraine. Korda and Kertész are constantly bombarded by offers from Italy and Germany, and not insignificant ones either, like where Kertész would be commissioned to direct the upcoming Henry Porter film, which is none other than the sequel to Anna Boleyn. Korda also started work on his new film, where the leads are played by his wife, Antónia Farkas and the Italian Capodzi. Szőreghy's latest work also turned out great.

I am now directing "Dracula", which I wrote with Mihály Kertész. The exterior scenes are almost completed. These were recorded around Helimental Melk. I intend to finish the interiors at the Corvin film-factory, because there isn't such a well equipped studio in Vienna. I'm coming back with the actors on the second of January. There are notable roles in the movie for Magda Sonja, Anna Marie, Hegener, Lene Myl, Paul Askonas. I'm bringing Vienna's best director of photography with me: Höss. The film has a grand concept, full of attractions. The winter landscapes will surely provide some first-class spectacle.

There is a historical reason behind the migration of these directors to Austria.

Hungary's film industry flourished during World War I, mostly thanks to a 1917 law — known as the "film-import ban"— which limited the number of foreign movies that could be distributed in the country. This ensured a huge appetite for domestic films, and helped create an infrastructure for film production that was on par with the best in the world, both from a technical and an artistic standpoint. This is the era in which the above mentioned Corvin film studio was built, with its iconic 40 meter (about 130 feet) long glass structure giving home to one of Europe's most state-of-the-art indoor stages.

The Corvin Film Studio

Unfortunately, when the import ban ended in 1919, the market was flooded with foreign films and the need for production dissipated, forcing filmmakers to seek work outside the country. *Dracula's Death* was made in this dire, uncertain environment. It was commissioned by the Lapa Film Studio in Vienna, and featured both Austrian and Hungarian actors.

The article above gives an interesting snapshot of the early stages of production. Lajthay refers to the movie simply as *Dracula* ("Drakula" in the original text, which is the common Hungarian spelling of the character's name), and not as *Dracula's Death* (*Drakula Halála*). He talks about co-writing the screenplay with Mihály Kertész (1886-1962), who was already a celebrated director in the 1910's, and who would go on to have a very successful career in the United States under the name Michael Curtiz. He is best remembered for directing *Casablanca*, for which he received an Academy Award in 1943. It is important to note that aside from this one interview, there is no other mention of Kertész's involvement with *Dracula's Death* in the years to come, and Károly Lajthay is always credited as the sole writer.

Austrian actor Paul Askonas (1879-1935) was chosen to play the title role. He was a member of the Deutsches Volkstheater (which roughly translates to "Theater for German-Speaking People") in Vienna, and his other films include *Three Tales of Terror* (1912) and *The Hands of Orlac* (1924).

Dracula's Death was not an adaptation of Bram Stoker's novel, but instead an original tale featuring the character. It told the story of Mary Land, a poor seamstress, who spends a night in a mental asylum following the death of her father, and this is where she encounters Dracula. He is either an immortal creature, or one of the patients who suffers from strange delusions…

Mary's role went to Margit Lux, a Hungarian actress born in 1902, who appeared in *The Devil* (1918), *The Magic Waltz* (1918), *Lu, The Coquette* (1919), and *The Nightmare* (1921). She was notably omitted from the first wave of articles covering the yet-to-be completed *Dracula's Death*.

Margit Lux in the Magic Waltz, 1918

A good example of her exclusion is a write-up in the pages of the Austrian magazine *Komödie (Comedy)*, from January 2, 1921:

KAROLY LAJTAY

— A NEW FILM —

The world of film will soon have to remember a new name, and this name is Károly Lajtay. He is both a movie director and an entrepreneur in one person. Lajtay comes from Budapest. He is not unknown in the film industry, since he has already had several directing successes in Budapest.

Therefore we are introducing Károly Lajtay to the valued readers of "Komödie". The urgent reason for this is that Lajtay has cast this new and enormous film with artists mostly from Vienna, and that the open-air scenes were shot in the surrounding areas of Wachau and Melk.

The subject of Lajtay's new film is named after a world-famous English novel and just as the novel, the movie will also be called "Dracula". This film will surely be a sensation.

Paul Askonas of Deutsches Volkstheater-fame was chosen for the male lead role. The movie features a new actress for the female lead — sure to bring great surprises — Lene Myl, whose photo was published in the previous issue of "Komödie". Lene Myl is a beautiful young blonde with great talent. She is a valuable discovery for cinema.

Next to these lead roles the movie also features Mr. Kutschera, Mr. Gotz and Ms. Waldow in important roles — also of Deutsches Volkstheater fame.

Recently Mr. Lajtay travelled to Budapest with his artists since there was no studio large enough in Vienna. The amazing interior shots were filmed in Budapest, in the Korwin-Film A. G. studio.

The Hungarian magazine *Képes Mozivilág (Illustrated World of Movies)* also names Lene Myl as the movie's female lead in their January 16, 1921 article:

Dracula — Károly Lajthay's latest film

It was about twenty years ago that Dracula, the most suspenseful and intriguing novel by English writer H. G. Wells, was serialized in Budapest Hirlap (Budapest Newspaper), and was later also published in book form. The novel drew great acclaim, because its gripping, twisted story captivated readers cover to cover. Károly Lajthay, the excellent Hungarian director, adapted the main plot of this novel into a film, as he is now working on the interior shots in Budapest, at the

Corvin studio. He will finish the indoor scenes this week, and will continue the exteriors at Wachau near Vienna, at Steinhof, and the area surrounding Melk. The female lead is played by a new star, Lene Myl, whose temperamental acting, sublime presence, and characteristic expression will ensure the movie's success. Lene Myl is from Serbia, her maiden name is Miléne Pavlovic. She's worked for film studios in Berlin and Romania, and she's been very successful in Vienna too, where she played one of the lead roles in Queen Draga.

Her partner: Paul Askenas, the member of the Deutsches Volkstheater in Vienna, and also Margit Lux, Elemér Thury, the great character-actor, as well as Dezső Zoltán, who is none other than Mihály Kertész's brother. We are eagerly awaiting the premiere of this sensational movie.

Accompanying the text are two publicity photos, one of Askonas, in his Dracula makeup, and the other is Lene Myl, credited as "the lead of Dracula".

Paul Askonas

Lene Myl

We have to acknowledge that this article contains an eye-catching mistake: it names H. G. Wells as the author of the novel *Dracula*, instead of Bram Stoker. As for Lene Myl's role in the movie: there could have been a casting change after the exterior shots were completed at the end of 1920, or the case may simply be that Myl played a smaller part, perhaps one of Dracula's wives. Or both of these could be true.

One of the most unique reports about the movie was published in the 1921 January issue of *Színház és Mozi (Theater and Cinema)*, in the form of a set visit at the Corvin studio during the shooting of Dracula's wedding. It clarifies some of the confusion surrounding the casting, and also provides some visual clues to the movie's look:

I ATTENDED A WEDDING

It wasn't one of the famous primadonnas who got wedded, and it wasn't one of our celebrated actors who got married, and I can't even say that one of our successful writers, poets, sculptors, or artists walked down the aisle, but I can still attest that I attended a wedding. First of all, because I really did, and secondly, because a wedding this interesting and strange has never been seen before.

I went to a wedding — at the Corvin filmstudio. The groom was no less than Asconas — as it turns out, he really is an artist — Vienna's favorite actor. The bride — but of course, a starlet — Margit Lux, the kind, talented actress, whose ability to cry on film already brought her great success.

So Asconas, who is no other than Dracula, a fantastic creature, like a modern Bluebeard, wants to bring a new woman to his magical castle, and this new woman is played by Margit Lux. He pulls every string possible to make the woman his, he summons the monasteries, spirits, different animals, and he is about to reach his goal, he already has her under his spell, when he glances at the cross hanging around her neck… and Dracula, this wondrous and mysterious creature, is powerless against the cross.

This is how Dracula's nuptials played out at the Corvin studios, and I probably don't even have to say it, but "Dracula" is a movie, and a sensational one at that, and its plot — precisely because it's quite intriguing — cannot be described here, so it can be more impactful when it arrives to the movie screens.

Dracula's wedding gives a taste of the film's energy. A huge room, marble all the way around, with a dark hallway at the center that appears to stretch forever. This is where Dracula resides, or more precisely, this is where he lives his mysterious life. It's night time. You can hear the sound of all kinds of animals yipping and squirming, and then a door opens in the middle, and beautiful women come to greet him, all in dreamy clothing, these were Dracula's current wives. But now he's awaiting his new bride, the most beautiful, the most desired, the one that he moved heaven and earth for, and the one who he showers with flowers when he sees…

How beautiful this will be on film — I thought to myself as I watched Dracula's shooting at the Corvin studio. Károly Lajthay worked day and night, tirelessly, so Dracula can properly greet his bride, and the scenes that he completed here will only make up a small portion of the four-act movie. What took an entire day's hard work will only last about five minutes on the screen. *The viewers, as they comfortably sit back on their lounge chairs, couldn't even imagine that the scenes that follow each other take so much incredible talent and work to rehearse, record, and compose.*

After the shoot I asked Lajthay about the upcoming movie, and this is what he had to say:

"These scenes are being produced for my latest film called "Dracula", which will be an epic, grandiose drama. We completed the exterior shots last month near Vienna. The interiors, as you can see, are being made now, at the Corvin studio, which is much better equipped than any in Vienna. The leads are played by Margit Lux, Lene Myl and Asconas.

This article is accompanied by two set photos, taken during the film's production. One shows Margit Lux and Dracula, and the other is of the above-mentioned wedding.

A detailed cast list was published in the introduction of the 1924 novelization of the movie:

DRACULA.....................................*Paul Askonas*

MARY...*Margit Lux*

GEORGE.......................................*Dezső Kertész*

THE CHIEF PHYSICIAN..................*Elemér Thury*

A FAKE SURGEON.........................*Lajos Rethey*

HIS ASSISTANT.............................*Aladár Ihász*

THE FUNNY LUNATIC...................*Karl Götz*

Additional roles played by Lajos Szalkay, Károly Hatvani, Oszkár Perczel, Béla Timár, Paula Kende and Lene Myl.

We know of two directors of photography who worked on the movie: Eduard Hösch and Lajos Gasser.

Even though the film didn't arrive in theaters until 1923, it was completed in 1921:

Karoly Lajthay, the excellent director who now resides in Vienna, completed the interior shots of his grand drama "Dracula" a few weeks ago at the Corvin film studio in Budapest. They just held the press premiere in Vienna, which was a great success.

This blurb, published in *Színház és Mozi* (*Theater and Cinema*), indicates that the movie had a showing sometime in 1921, although it refers to a press screening that was probably not open to the general public.

After this, Dracula's Death unceremoniously disappears from the pages of the periodicals for almost two years. The most likely explanation is that the movie failed to find a distributor (considering the state of the Hungarian film market, this is not all that surprising) and without it, the promotional campaign came to a screeching halt.

Still, something significant did happen in the year between the completion and the release of the film: Dracula arrived at the theaters…

F. W. Murnau's *Nosferatu: A Symphony of Horror* proved to be quite a sensation when it was released in Hungary in the fall of 1922 under the title *Dracula*. The critics raved about its "occult thrills", and audiences flocked to the cinemas to see Max Scherck's outstanding performance. "*The Dracula-fever is rising.*" — said *Színházi Élet* (*Theater Life* — 1922/45) in its film review, and it's possible that this newfound interest in the character is what helped *Dracula's Death* finally get picked up by a distributor.

It also appears to be the reason why the movie was renamed, since up to this point Lajthay's film was also called *Dracula*.

Ad for Drakula (Nosferatu)

Eventually Jenő Tuchten's Filmdistribution Company purchased the movie in 1923. Censorship records tell us that it was made up of 1448 meters of film, it was a drama in 4 acts, and it was made in 1921 by the Lapa Film Studio.

Jenő Tuchten's company promoted the film with a clever ad that was designed to look like a birth announcement:

We are honored to let everyone who is interested know that we acquired the Hungarian film industry's latest product — and pride-, DRACULA'S DEATH, a film attraction in 5 parts, and we will distribute it. In a few weeks it will premiere in one of the capital city's film theaters, which we would like to bring to the trade's attention.

Jenő Tuchten's Filmdistribution Company, as the adopter.
Károly Lajthay, the parent
Margit Lux and Paul Askonas
As the leads.
Karl Götz, Paula Kende
Lene Myl, Dezső Kertész
Elemér Thury, Károly Hatvani
Lajos Kéthey, Lajos Szalkai
Oszkár Perczel, Aladár Ihász
Béla Timár, as the cast

The following rather charming article describes the industry's excitement surrounding the film's release in *Színházi Élet* (*Theater Life* — 4/8/1923):

POSTAL CAMPAIGN ON DOHÁNY STREET

Those bohemians who get their breakfast and lunch at the New York Cafe have been surprised by the unusual rushing-around that's been taking place at the corner of Dohány Street and Erzsébet Boulevard. Bicycle carriers arrive at building 57, just as others are leaving. As if a large international conference was taking place there, where it was necessary to send out a telegram report every minute. But the only telegrams at Jenő Tuchten's company are the ones arriving en masse are from the movie exhibitors who have heard the news: the excellent distributor will show the sensational Lajthay film, Dracula's Death, at the Tivoli theater on April 28. The movie deals with Dracula's spine-chilling legend with groundbreaking special effects, so it is in the center of the industry's attention, which hopes that it will become this spring season's great success.

The first known public exhibition of the film took place in the Hungarian city of Nyíregyháza. It played at the Városi Mozgó Színház (City Motion Theater) for three days, March 21-23, 1923, as a double feature with *How Could You, Jean?* (under the Hungarian title *Önagysága a Mindenes...*), the Mary Pickford-helmed American comedy from 1918.

The local distributor must have been worried about audiences confusing *Dracula's Death* with *Nosferatu* — which played there just a few months prior — because the theater ran the following clarification in *Nyírvidék* (*Nyír-region* 1923/3/22), the local newspaper:

DRACULA'S DEATH IS NOT THE SAME as the Dracula that was recently exhibited in Nyiregyhaza. It is the latest great product of the newly reinvigorated Hungarian film industry, it's suspenseful, and its plot covers the original English novel.

Nyírvidék (*Nyír-region*) also published an advertisement that tried to present the movie as a solely Hungarian production, going as far as omitting every foreign actor from its cast listing, including the lead Paul Askonas.

Dracula's Death: the first suspenseful adventure film of the recently reinvigorated Hungarian film industry. Starring: Lux Margit, Thury Elemér, Szalkay Lajos, and many other famous and well-known Hungarian actors.

The film's formal premiere was on April 28, 1923, at the Tivoli Theater in Budapest — although one source, the magazine *Mozi és Film* (*Theater and Film* — 1923/23) puts that date on April 14.

By this point the promotional campaign was back on, and a number of periodicals published reviews and advertisements for the big event.

On the pages of *Szinházi Élet* (*Theater Life*), 1923/13:

WHOSE DEATH EVERYBODY'S INTERESTED IN...

Dracula is the hero of mysterious twilight, grim nights and unnamed terrors, whose legendary vampire was watched by hundreds of thousands at the cinema, and who will soon be back on the movie screens. Karoly Lajthay, the noted director who immigrated to Germany and who has already made several successful films, adapts this rather effective story in a new and original way, under the title "Dracula's Death". In his hands, Dracula isn't a vision, but a living-breathing person, who is kept as a lunatic in an insane asylum. And this is the asylum where a young girl arrives with her fiance on a Christmas night to visit her dying father. This is where Dracula and the young girl meet, and fight a blood-curdling battle. He takes her to his terrifying, crumbling castle, and it's in this frightening and torturous setting where the monster tries to finish his victim. Following the most suspenseful adventures, her fiance reaches the castle, to save his love from the deadly kiss at the very last minutes. And Dracula, whose demonic soul lives in a mortal body after all, is made to pay for his evil deeds with the bullet of a revolver...

This grand film, which was mostly shot around the snow-covered mountains of Transylvania, is brought to the Budapest market by Jeno Tuchten's film-lending company, and will be first shown at the Tivoli. Aside from the interesting and twisting storylines, another strength of the movie is Margit Lux, the excellent, young actress, who hasn't been seen in any productions for the last two years. And Dracula is played by Paul Askonas, who is considered by the Germans to be one of their most nuanced actors. Interesting is that his mask has been commissioned though a half-million forint competition, in which almost every theatrical makeup designer participated. Those who already had a chance to see the mask say that they couldn't even imagine anything more mystical or disturbing.

This particular article mentions the "mask" (today we would call it special effects makeup) worn by Askonas. We did get one glimpse of the actor as Dracula in a promotional still published in *Kepes Mozivilag* (*Illustrated World of Movies*) back in 1921, but this confirms that he altered his appearance in order to transform into the character.

While there are slight inconsistencies between the different articles, they do touch on the same general plot elements. Mary spends a night in a mental asylum, where Dracula kidnaps her in the middle of the night and takes her to his castle. He is an otherworldly creature who wants to make her his newest wife, but the cross hanging from her neck repels him at the last minute. At the end, she wakes up: the terrifying ordeal was nothing but a dream.

In *Pesti Hírlap* (*Pest Newspaper*) 1923-04-28:

TIVOLI'S BIG PREMIERE
DRACULA'S DEATH, DRAMA IN 5 PARTS

Dracula's Death has a suspenseful, thrilling plot. After the secrets of the asylum, the devil takes the viewer to his castle. It's a fantastical tale. The seduced girl is saved by the cross. The devil is afraid of the burning incense. The cross is victorious against the deceitful. We don't usually reveal the movie's tricks, but so the tense scenes won't harm the viewer, we'll let you in on the secret that half of the scenes are part of a dream. But an interesting dream.

The following article appeared in several different newspapers — *Pesti Hírlap (Pest Newspaper)* 1923-04-27, *Budapest Hírlap (Budapest Newspaper)* 1923-04-28, *8 Órai Újság* (8 O'Clock Paper) 1923-04-28*)* — which suggests that it was written as promotional material (perhaps by the distributor), and may be more akin to a press release than a traditional review.

BIG PREMIERE AT THE TIVOLI

Dracula's Death, a drama in 5 acts — which was written and directed by Karoly Lajthay, based on the world famous novel — is captivating with its exciting and suspenseful plot. Mary, the poor seamstress, travels from an idyllic village in the Alpine to a city asylum, where her father is kept. Here, she meets a madman who claims to be Dracula, the immortal, and that he lives in an infernal castle surrounded by otherworldly pleasures. Mary has to stay a night at the asylum and she dreams of Dracula. The visions of this dream are brought to the screen with fantastic imagery. Dracula takes the girl to his castle where they're preparing for a wedding. Mary defends herself against the wicked temptation with the cross hanging around her neck. Then the devil and the cross battle for several different scenes. At last she wakes up from her dream, and true love prevails: her fiance comes for her. Foreign and local actors bring this interesting tale to life: Margit Lux, Paul Askins, Karl Gotz, Dezso Kertesz, Lajos Rethey, Paula Kende, Lene Myl, Elemer Thury, etc.

A novelization of the movie was published in 1924 by Lajos Pánczél (1897-1971), an acclaimed film journalist, as issue six in a series of Filmbooks, or "fantastical film-novels". When compared to the reviews published in the periodicals, it appears to be quite faithful to the events

Lajos Pánczél

in the movie. Unfortunately the author of the book is unknown, since the only credit within the publication's pages belongs to Pánczél himself, as the series' editor.

He launched Filmbooks in 1921, and the series went on to have several dozen issues. The only clue as to the creative team behind it comes from a newspaper blurb from *Színházi Élet* (*Theater Life* — 1921/8), at the announcement of the first installment, which was based on the movie *Madame Dubarry*. It lists the following authors as contributors: Lajos Pánczél, Dezső Váczi, Andor Lajta and Ernő Ágoston, and it also names the cover artist, Andor Kolozsvári. We can't be sure that this team stayed with the series, or if this is applicable to *Dracula's Death* in any way, but at least we learn that Pánczél worked with other writers on some of these novelizations.

The book was cataloged at the National Széchényi Library on May 27, 1924, and the film's writer-director, Károly Lajthay was entered into records as its author.

At this point, *Dracula's Death* seems to have disappeared from the public discourse. Still, it's impossible to tell what — if any — impact it had on audiences at the time. While it wasn't the sensation that the Jenő Tuchten's Filmdistribution Company hoped for, there are some signs that the movie lingered in the cultural memory for at least a couple more years. Almost a decade later, a 1931 issue of Újság (*Newspaper*, 10-15-1931) makes a point to mention Dracula when it reports Lajthay's visit to Budapest:

Károly Lajthay, the excellent Hungarian post-war director who has made several successful movies both at home and abroad — for example, he was the first one to adapt Dracula to film — is back in Budapest for a few days, as he's in negotiations to make two talkies.

Lajthay's *Dracula* gets another mention in a 1942 edition of *Filmlexicon*, which states that "*Dracula* was a great success", and that it was a movie Lajthay "directed in Berlin". The first statement regarding the film's success is questionable, but the second about Berlin being a shooting location is almost certainly false.

After this, *Dracula's Death* truly faded into obscurity, until its existence was rediscovered in the 1990s.

* * *

There are many reasons why silent movies like *Dracula's Death* haven't survived.

For example, in the early decades of the 20th century, film stocks were made with cellulose nitrate, an extremely flammable plastic. It was even known to ignite spontaneously under certain circumstances, and several infamous vault fires (Fox in 1937, MGM in 1965) are a testament to how dangerous it was. While films made of different materials existed, they were less flexible and much harder to work with, so it remained the industry standard until the late 1940's, when Kodak finally introduced a safe and comparable alternative. Another huge factor in the demise of early films is that they required climate controlled (low temperature, low humidity) storage in order to prevent the onset of irreversible decay. Without these measures, film will quite literally crumble into dust over time.

The destruction of European cities during World War II is often considered another factor, which certainly played a role, although not to the extent one might expect. Let's consider that American silent films fared only slightly better than their European counterparts, and the continental US was not only spared during the war, but the studios that made these movies are still located on the exact same lots in Hollywood as they were back then. This is remarkable stability over the course of a century.

The single most significant reason for the disappearance of silent films was the lack of effort to preserve them. They lost all of their commercial value once sound was introduced to the movies: audiences no longer had any interest in seeing them, so there was simply no incentive to hold onto them. Instead of continuing their difficult and expensive storage, they were often recycled for the plastic they contained: in Hungary, most films were turned into bags. While some individual studios and private collectors attempted to rescue them, there wasn't any institutional body that would take on this responsibility until it was much too late.

The Institute of Theatre and Film Science (Színház és Filmtudományi Intézet) was established in 1957, more than half a century after the first Hungarian film, *The Dance (A Tánc)* was made in 1901. By then, it was impossible to make up for the lost time. To date, despite the tireless efforts of film historians, only 7% of Hungarian silent films have been recovered.

The fact that the Dracula's Death novelization still exists today is a great example of the importance of archiving. Its only known surviving copy wasn't found in a private collection, in an attic, or in a forgotten corner of an antique bookstore, but on the shelves of the National Széchényi Library (Országos Széchényi Könyvtár). It was founded in 1802 with the explicit mission to preserve Hungary's written heritage, and to this day, publishers are mandated to provide a copy of every single work released in the country. Most articles quoted in this essay also survived because of this preservation measure, since the library collects periodicals as well.

An interesting anecdote is that the book almost didn't make it into the archives. Lajos Pánczél published Dracula's Death in the city of Timişoara (Temesvár), which by 1924 was part of Romania, and not Hungary, and presumably for this reason Pánczél neglected to submit a copy. However, the books themselves were printed in Budapest (at the

Jókai and Ibli Press), and on this technicality the National Széchényi Library filed an official complaint against the publisher. Only after this warning was Dracula's Death submitted.

It is only because of the library's persistence that we can read the novelization today.

* * *

One important question remains: is there any chance that Dracula's Death, the movie, somehow survived? Could it be out there, in somebody's basement, attic, or collecting dust in a warehouse somewhere? It seems like every couple of years there is a new discovery of a film thought to be long lost, so… could Lajthay's movie be next?

Unlikely, but *not* entirely impossible.

The era of finding forgotten films in attics seems to be over, partly because by now they would be far too deteriorated, but also because of the considerable efforts made in recent decades to uncover them. So if a copy of Dracula's Death is still out there, it has most likely been already collected, and just hasn't been identified yet.

There are several reasons why it would be difficult to recognize any movie from this time period. To start with, it's *extremely* improbable that a copy of a complete film was overlooked for so long, so if anything survived, it's most likely just a fragment. A single scene, a small section of film, or if we're lucky, maybe a reel. This would mean that the footage might be completely out of context.

Silent movies pose an additional challenge by not having sound, because without the language spoken by the actors it's often impossible to even tell their country of origin. Film historians might be able to narrow a region down based on costumes or exterior locations, but even that takes a lot of work. Sometimes actors are recognized, or a motif or prop gives a clue to the story being told. This is real detective work.

That is why it's important that the Dracula's Death novelization is available in English, so archivists outside of Hungary can be familiar with its plot. This way they can correctly identify moments that don't obviously belong to the first ever Dracula film: a young couple decorating a Christmas tree. A horse drawn sleigh rushing through a snowy landscape. Two madmen attempting to perform eye surgery on a helpless girl. Even Dracula himself might be difficult to recognize, since in parts of the story he's depicted as a lunatic wearing a royal cloak, arguing with patients in an asylum courtyard. Not exactly our mental image of the famous vampire.

There aren't a lot of records indicating that the movie travelled outside the country — although it was shown in Austria at one point — but there are plenty of examples of collectors selling and trading old films across border lines. It only takes one copy...

This is, of course, just wishful thinking. The odds are truly against Lajthay's Dracula, and the sad reality is that it will most likely never be seen by modern audiences. On the other hand, there is still a lot to discover. The story of silent films is far from over.

So if not Dracula, then maybe something else will emerge from the vaults of the many film archives around the world. Maybe we'll finally get a glimpse of the silver screen's first werewolf, or the first Dr. Jekyll, or the first Phantom. Who knows, one day we might even get to see Lon Chaney's vampire step out of the fog onto the cobblestone-covered streets of London.

As the Hungarian saying goes: hope dies last.

THE END

ACKNOWLEDGEMENTS

I want to thank József Sváb for creating the stunning illustrations that brought *Dracula's Death* to life.

This book — quite literally — would not have been possible without the important archival work done at the National Széchényi Library in Hungary. I would like to especially thank István Elbe and Zita Szatmári-Lévai for their generosity and support. I had the opportunity to interview Mr. Elbe in the spring of 2019, and that conversation started me on a year-long journey that led to the writing of this book.

I would like to thank Jenő Farkas, Hungary's leading Dracula scholar, for assisting me in my research. His contribution to the study of *Dracula's Death* can not be overstated. His book *Dracula and the Vampires* (*Drakula és a Vámpírok* — 2010) is perhaps the most comprehensive publication written about both the historical and the fictional Dracula, and I hope that English-speaking audiences will someday have an opportunity to read it.

Márton Kurutz from the National Film Institute and Film Archives helped me better understand the history of silent films in Hungary.

Gyöngyi Balogh was kind enough to answer my many tedious questions about the silent film era.

Athena Buell gave *The Devil Flew Away* the academic fine tuning it needed.

My wife, Dr. Tiffany E. Tamasfi, read the book with a keen editorial eye.

I would like to acknowledge Gary D. Rhodes' 2010 essay *Drakula halála (1921): The Cinema's First Dracula*, which is not only an excellent resource on the film's history, but it also contains the first English language translation of *Dracula's Death*, by Péter Litván and Gary D. Rhodes.

And last, but definitely not least, I want to thank Erika Romero for editing this book. The original Hungarian novelization has a very unique, old-timey, often strange flair, and I'm grateful that she helped me translate it into English. If you enjoyed reading *Dracula's Death*, it is because of her hard work.

László Tamásfi